Underpants Are Awesome!

Three Pants-tastic Books in One!

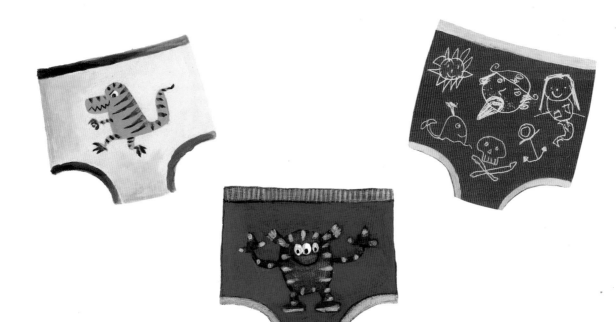

Claire Freedman and Ben Cort

SIMON & SCHUSTER

London New York Sydney Toronto New Delhi

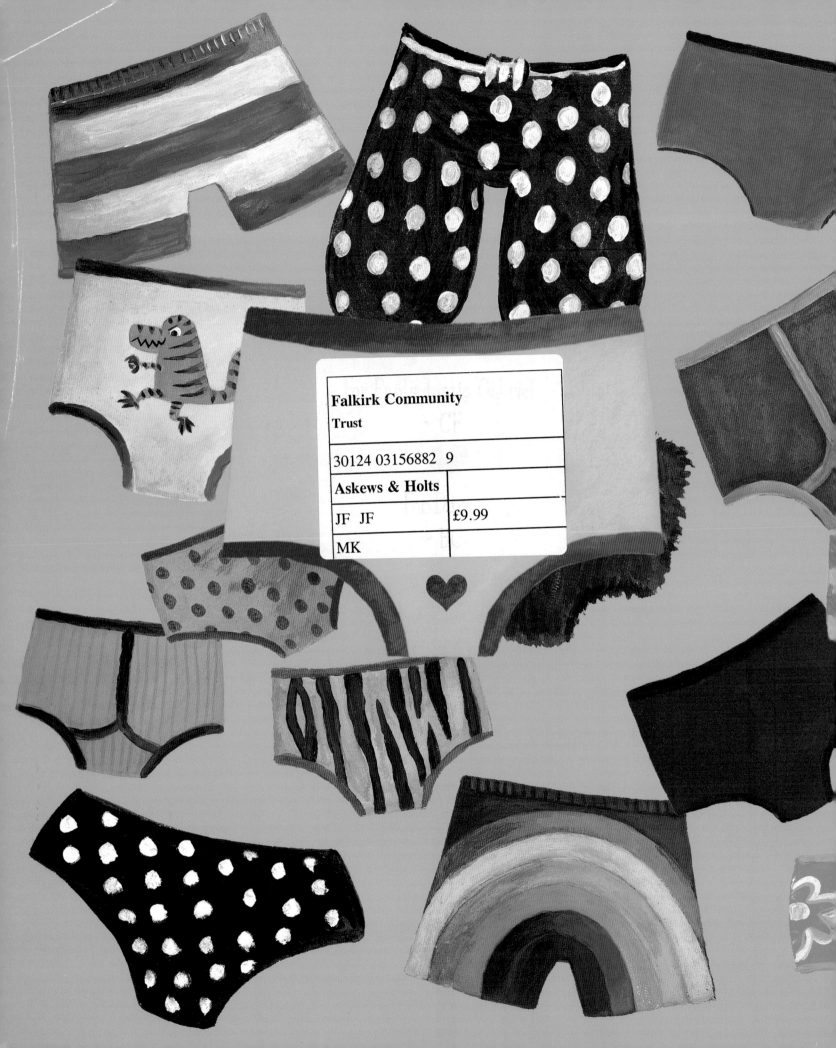

Dinosaurs Love Underpants

Dinosaurs were all wiped out,
A long way back in history,
No one knows quite how or why,
Now this book solves the mystery . . . .

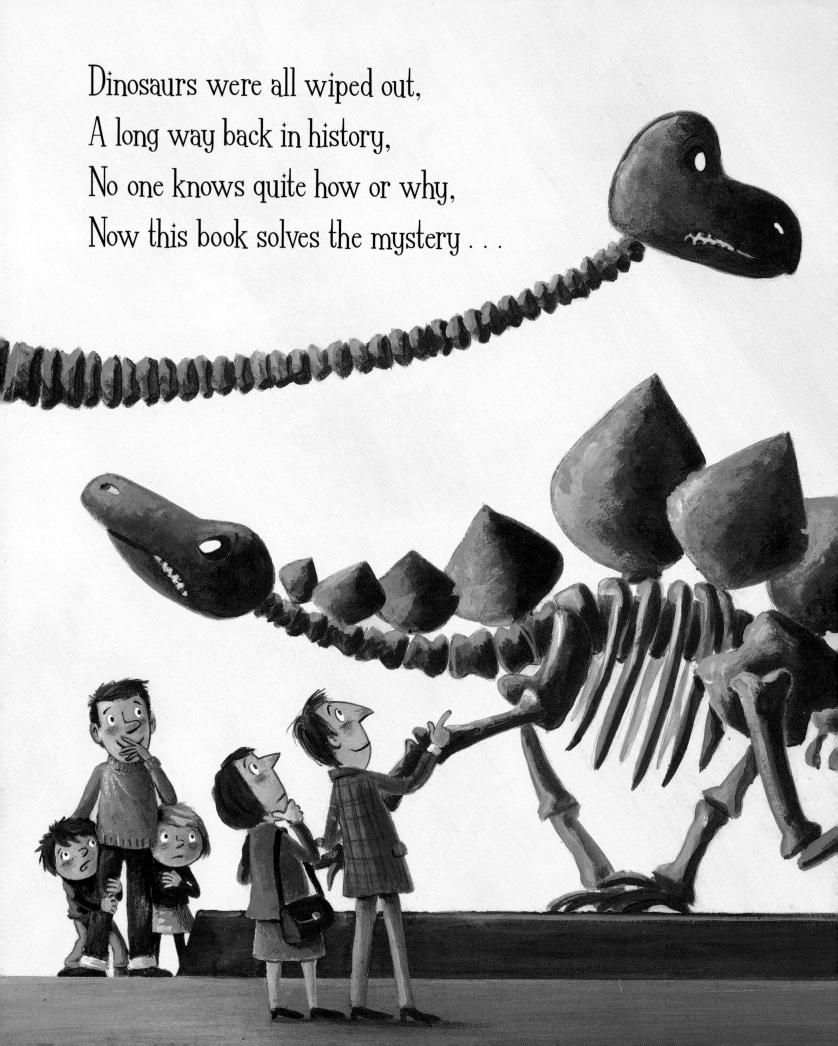

It all began when cavemen,
Felt embarrassed in the nude,
So someone dreamt up underpants,
To stop them looking rude.

The dinosaurs roamed everywhere,
All teeth and huge long necks,
But scariest and meanest,
Was Tyrannosaurus rex!

When T-rex saw Man's knickers,
He roared with deafening rants,
"I don't want to eat you up,
I want your underpants!"

T-rex pinched a furry pair,
But his pants quickly ripped,
He couldn't get them past his feet,
Oh! Whoops! Watch out! He tripped!

Triceratops was happy,
Wearing pants on every horn,
Till Styracosaurus snatched them,
And they ended up all torn.

The pants from Woolly Mammoth coats,
Made Stegosaurus itchy,
Diplodocus was really cross,
His pants were far too titchy!

"We've too few knickers to go around!"
The cavemen quaked in shock,
"These dinos are pants crazy,
They've completely run amok!"

Soon pants were flying everywhere,
All slit by tooth and claw,
The dinosaurs were fighting,
In a great pants tug-of-war.

The Mighty Pants War raged all night,
THUMP, POW, BASH, THWACK, CLOUT!
The fighting got so crazy,
All the dinos were wiped out!

The next day, out the cavemen crept,
And cheered at what they saw,
"Hooray! Our biggest enemy,
Is now at last no more!"

So when you put your pants on,
Always treat them with great care,
Pants and knickers saved Mankind,
They're not just underwear!

To Michael, Ich liebe Dich

~ CF

♥

For Matilda, with love

~ BC

♥

Aliens in Underpants Save the World

Aliens love underpants,
It's lucky that they do,
For pants helped save our universe,
Sounds crazy, but it's true!

On one pants-pinching mission,
As the aliens zoomed through space,
Their spaceships shook and wobbled,
Ooooh! Their hearts began to race.

Their radars bleeped, their sirens wailed,
On came the warning light!
Yikes! Heading straight for planet Earth,
Was one huge meteorite!

Meanwhile, on Earth, the scientists,
Had such an awful fright.
"What's THAT?" they gulped in horror,
"Picked up on our satellite?"

The fire engines came racing,
Police and air rescue too,
But with just four hours till impact,
There was little they could do!

Quick! Down to Earth the aliens shot,
And jumped out with a shout,
"No time to lose, if Earth blows up,
Our pants supply runs out!"

They took pants down from washing lines,
And raided knicker stores,
They sneaked inside our houses,
And pulled bloomers out of drawers.

The aliens stitched the underwear,
And proudly they unfurled,
The most GINORMOUS pair of pants,
Made in the whole wide world!

Wheee! Whizzing in their spaceships,
They stretched out the pants in place,
And as the meteor landed – PING!
It zoomed back into space!

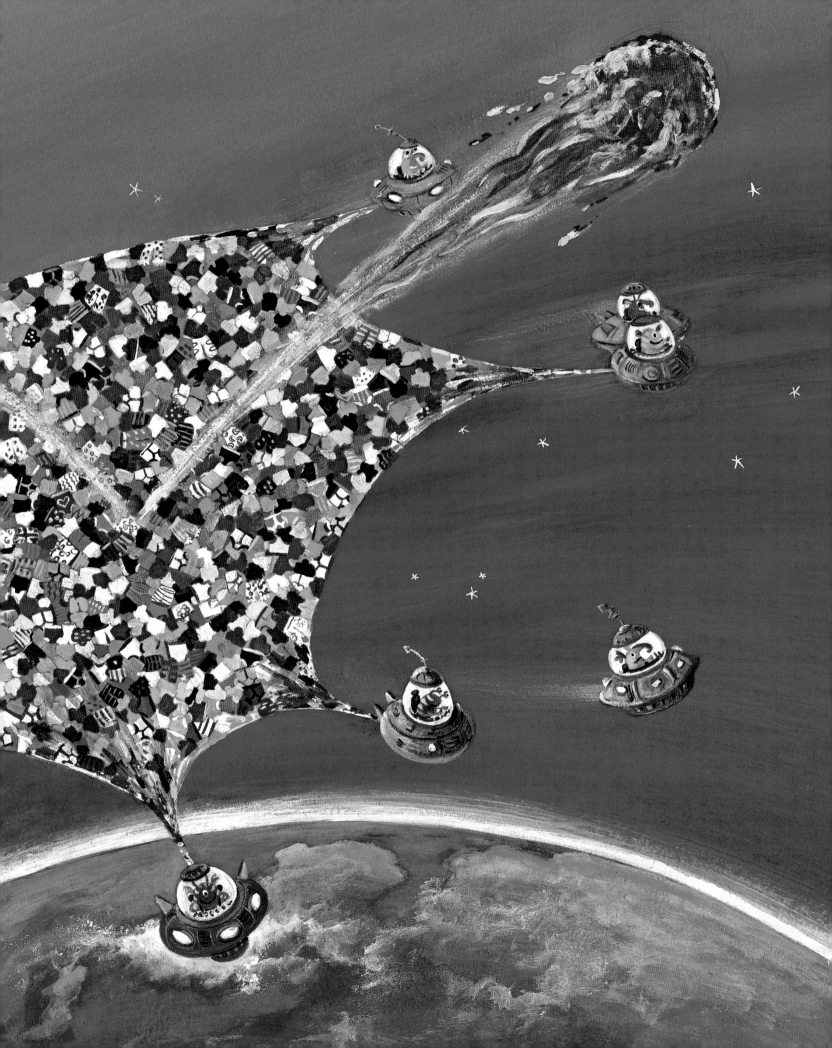

"The meteorite has vanished!"
Gasped the people in surprise,
"We thought we saw huge underpants,
But can't believe our eyes!"

Back home the aliens all cheered,
"Our pants plan was fantastic,
We saved the Earth and underpants,
With pingy pants elastic!"

So should your pants go missing,
There's no need to make a fuss,
Let the aliens have their fun
They've done SO much for us!

For My Michael – with all my love x
~ CF

For Nicole Ivett – a real treasure!
~ BC

Pirates Love Underpants

These pirates SO love underpants,
They're on a special quest
To find the fabled Pants of Gold,
For the Captain's treasure chest.

"Anchors aweigh!" the Captain cries,
"Hoist up Black Bloomer's sail!
Unfurl the secret treasure map,
Pants pirates NEVER fail!"

Black Bloomer bobs upon the waves,
The Captain shouts, "Hooray!
Sharks in fancy UNDERPANTS,
We've found Big Knickers Bay!"

The pirates grab their cutlasses,
And row their boats to shore.
But, "Yikes, me hearties, what is this?
Someone's been 'ere before!"

The footprints lead through shifting dunes,
Across the Three Pants Ridge.
Snap! Snap! snarl hungry crocodiles,
Beneath the Long-John Bridge!

The pirates wade through gurgling swamps,
Through caves as black as night.
They trek through prickly undergrowth,
Then, GULP! Oh, what a sight!

"We're here too late!" the pirates gasp.
"ANOTHER pirate crew!
They've found the golden underpants.
What are we going to do?"

The Captain has a cunning plan.
It's clever! It's fantastic!
"Grab their fancy underpants and . . .
CUT through the elastic!"

Sshh! As the rival pirates sleep,
They SNIP round on tip-toe.
But help! The Captain's parrot SQUAWKS,
And wakes them up – Oh no!

"Grab those pants!" the Captain roars.
"They're after us – oooh-arrr!"
But with their pants around their feet,
They don't get very far!

"Yo-ho! Ho-ho!" the pirates dance,
"Fine treasure fills our hold,
But what's the booty we love best?
The glittering PANTS OF GOLD!"

So when you put your pants on, CHECK,
The elastic is in place.
Or like those silly pirates found –
You'll have a bright red face!

Look out for more pants-tastic adventures from Claire Freedman and Ben Cort!

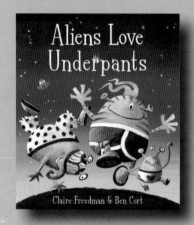
Aliens Love Underpants
Claire Freedman & Ben Cort

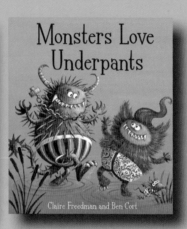
Monsters Love Underpants
Claire Freedman and Ben Cort

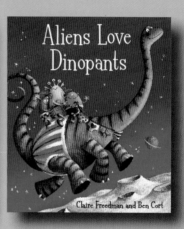
Aliens Love Dinopants
Claire Freedman and Ben Cort

Aliens Love Panta Claus
Claire Freedman and Ben Cort

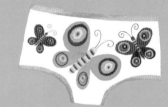

SIMON & SCHUSTER

This collection first published in Great Britain in 2022 by Simon & Schuster UK Ltd
1st Floor, 222 Gray's Inn Road, London, WC1X 8HB

Dinosaurs Love Underpants published in 2008
Aliens in Underpants Save the World published in 2009
Pirates Love Underpants published in 2012

A CIP catalogue record for this book is available from the British Library

PB 978-1-3985-1143-9 • eBook 978-1-3985-1144-6

Printed in China

13 5 7 9 10 8 6 4 2

FSC
www.fsc.org

MIX
Paper from
responsible sources
FSC® C020056